#5

SOCCER 'CATS

Matt Christopher®

Master of Disaster

Text by Stephanie Peters

Illustrated by Daniel Vasconcellos

LITTLE, BROWN AND COMPANY

New York ✤ An AOL Time Warner Company

To Barbara, Mark, Tim, and Renee

First Paperback Edition

Library of Congress Cataloging-in-Publication Data

Peters, Stephanie.
    Master of Disaster / [by Matt Christopher] ; text by Stephanie Peters ; illustrated by Daniel Vasconcellos. —1st ed.
        p.   cm.—(Soccer Cats ; #5)
    Summary: When Jason, the team clown, finds that he will be taking the regular goalie's place in an upcoming soccer game, he embarks on a determined plan to learn everything he can about goalkeeping.
    ISBN 0-316-13555-0 (hc)/ISBN 0-316-16498-4 (pb)
    [1. Soccer—Fiction.] I. Vasconcellos, Daniel, ill.   II. Title.

PZ7.P441833 Mas2001
[Fic]—dc21   00-033046

                    HC: 10 9 8 7 6 5 4 3 2 1
                    PB: 10 9 8 7 6 5 4 3 2 1

                            WOR (hc)

                          COM-MO (pb)

                Printed in the United States of America

Soccer 'Cats Team Roster

Lou Barnes	*Striker*
Jerry Dinh	*Striker*
Stookie Norris	*Striker*
Dewey London	*Halfback*
Bundy Neel	*Halfback*
Amanda Caler	*Halfback*
Brant Davis	*Fullback*
Lisa Gaddy	*Fullback*
Ted Gaddy	*Fullback*
Alan Minter	*Fullback*
Bucky Pinter	*Goalie*

Subs:

Jason Shearer

Dale Tuget

Roy Boswick

Edith "Eddie" Sweeny

Chapter 1

Jason Shearer popped a piece of gum into his mouth, then bent over to tighten the laces on his sneakers. Soccer practice was about to start.

"Hey, Jason, got any more gum?" Dale Tuget looked hopeful.

Jason fished around in his pocket and came up empty-handed. "Wait a minute," he said, tapping his chin. "I do have a piece of ABC gum. Want that?"

Dale shrugged. "Okay."

Jason spit out the gum he'd been chewing and held it out to Dale. "Here you go!"

Dale shrank back. "Yuck! That gum's already been chewed!"

Jason stuck the gum back in his mouth. "Exactly! It's ABC gum — *Already Been Chewed*! Get it?" He slapped his leg and laughed.

"Dale! Jason!" The voice of their coach boomed behind them. "Stop horsing around and get ready for warm-ups."

Dale and Jason hurried to join the other Soccer 'Cats on the field.

The Soccer 'Cats were playing the Panthers in a week. The Panthers were a tough team. Coach Bradley planned to work on some plays for the game.

"I'll need your full concentration today, 'Cats," he said as he set out cones and balls. "But let's loosen up with some drills first."

The 'Cats formed two lines. One after the other, they dribbled as quickly as possible

2

through the cones, then shot on the goal. After ten minutes of this, they moved on to a passing drill, then a passing drill with defense in place. Bucky Pinter, the team's starting goalie, was in one goal. Jason volunteered to go in the other, and the drill began.

Jason kept up a steady stream of chatter as each player came toward him.

"First up is Stookie Norris. They say Stookie's got a shot so sweet he should change his name to Cookie. He weaves, he shoots, he — oh, oh, he misses! Well, that's the way the cookie crumbles!"

Stookie growled. Jason laughed.

"Dewey London takes a turn. Hmmm, Dewey or don't we think he'll be able to outfox this goalie?" Jason did a little jig and repeated in a singsong voice, "Dewey or don't we? Dewey or don't we?" Dewey, distracted, tripped and fell. Jason called out gleefully, "Guess, we don't, Dewey?"

"Knock it off, Jason," Dewey said, getting up and brushing off his shorts.

Jason raised an eyebrow. "But this is my tried-and-true method of goalkeeping!"

"Tried-and-true, my foot!" Stookie Norris sneered. "You hardly ever stop a ball in practice, and I don't think you've ever been in a game as goalie. It's a good thing, too, for our team record's sake!"

Jason was about to retort when a hand on his shoulder stopped him.

"May I have a word with you?"

Chapter 2

Coach Bradley was standing behind him.

"Uh, sure, Coach. Of course."

Coach Bradley led him a few paces away from the goal.

"I don't think you're taking practice too seriously today."

Jason looked sheepish. "Aw, I was only kidding around."

Coach Bradley gazed at him for a long moment. "Jason, I know I haven't worked much with you on goalkeeping techniques. If you like, I'll take some time after practice today to show you a thing or two."

Jason was looking forward to playing computer games after practice, so he decided to fib. "That's okay, Coach. I've been paying attention to what you've been telling Bucky, so I know what to do."

"That's good," the coach said, "because you're the starting goalie for the next few games."

Jason blinked. "What?" he squeaked. "What about Bucky?"

"Bucky is going on vacation. So I'm glad you've been listening." Coach Bradley patted him on the shoulder, then turned his attention to the rest of the team.

Hoo boy, Jason thought. His stomach did a flip-flop at the thought of being in the goal for a whole game. And the first game would be against the Panthers!

"Hey, Jason, you look like you just saw a

ghost," said Dale as Jason walked by him. Jason didn't reply.

In fact, Jason didn't say another word for the rest of practice. As one ball after another soared past him and into the net, he began to realize how little he knew about being a goalie.

Jason was picking at his dinner that night when the telephone rang. It was Dale.

"What happened to you during practice?" Dale asked.

Jason explained about Bucky's vacation. Dale whistled.

"So you get to be starting goalie, huh? Well, I'll miss you on the bench."

"Keep my seat warm for me," Jason said dejectedly. "I'm sure I'll be back beside you before halftime."

"Why don't you ask the coach to give you some extra help?" Dale asked.

Jason cleared his throat. "Ah, I sort of told

him I knew what I was doing. How can I go to him now and tell him I really don't?"

"Well, then let's get a book from the library or find a Web site that explains how to play goalie. Maybe reading about it will help you master it."

"Oh, I'll be the master all right," Jason replied glumly. "Master of disaster, that is."

Chapter 3

The next morning, Dale sat in front of the computer in his bedroom, hands poised over the keys. Jason stood behind him.

"So, how do we do this?" Jason asked.

Dale gave him a surprised look. "Haven't you ever gone online before?"

Jason shook his head. "We're not hooked up to the Internet yet."

"Well, it's pretty easy," Dale said. He typed in a few commands to get to the World Wide Web, then paused. "It's sort of like using a dictionary or an encyclopedia. You tell the computer what you want to know, and it searches for it. It finds you a list of Web sites that have to do with your topic. Let's try searching under the word *soccer*." He typed some more. Within moments, a long list of soccer Web sites appeared.

Jason groaned. "Are we going to have to look at every one of those?"

Dale laughed. "Nah, we'll ask the computer to look for something a little more specific. Let's try *soccer goalkeeper*." This time, the list was shorter. Dale scrolled the screen down slowly so he and Jason could read the entries.

Dale tapped the screen. "This looks good!" He moved the cursor with the mouse and clicked to call up the site.

As Jason watched, the screen changed until it looked like a page from a soccer magazine.

"Cool!" Jason said enthusiastically. "So where's the info on how to be the best goalie ever?"

Dale moved the mouse again and clicked on the word *goalkeeper*. The soccer screen was replaced by another screen, this time filled with images of famous goalkeepers.

Dale drummed his fingers on the desk. "Says here you can click on one of these pictures and get tips from the goalies themselves on how to improve your play. Wanna try one?"

Jason pointed to one picture. "I recognize her. Let's try her first."

Dale clicked on the picture. A new screen appeared. Both boys read silently.

After a moment, Jason sighed. "Do you understand any of this?"

Dale shook his head. "Not really. Let's try another goalkeeper."

But the next one wasn't much help, either. Neither were the two after that. "I think these might be for people who already know the basics of playing goalie," Jason said finally.

"That's not me." He slumped down on Dale's bed.

"There are lots of other sites we could try," Dale offered.

"Yeah, but who has the time to read through them all to find the right one?" Jason complained. "Besides, even if we did find a good one, how could I learn from it? It'd be stuck inside your computer."

Dale logged off the computer and the screen went black. "We can always try the library," he suggested.

Jason shoved off the bed. "I guess it can't hurt. Let's go."

At the library, they searched the sports-book section until they found a simple beginner's guide to goalkeeping. Jason checked it out and they headed back to Dale's house.

The two boys flopped onto Dale's bed and read the book start to finish. When they were both done, Jason rolled onto his back and stared at the ceiling.

"I'm doomed. There's no way I can learn to do all that stuff by the game," he said dismally. "I can hear it now: 'Ladies and gentlemen, introducing today's goalie, Jason Shearer, the Master of Disaster himself.'"

Chapter 4

Jason left Dale's house with the book under his arm. Dale gave him a weak thumbs-up.

"I'm doomed," Jason repeated to himself. On the way home, he passed a playground. It was near lunchtime, so the place was practically empty. Only two kids were there.

One of the kids had a basketball. She was doing some kind of drill where she'd dribble up to the hoop, stop, then toss the ball toward the basket. Jason stopped to watch.

Man, he thought after a minute, *she must*

have the worst shot in the world. She hasn't made one yet!

Then he realized that she wasn't practicing her shooting, she was practicing her rebounding. Jason watched for a minute longer, then turned to look at the other kid.

The kid was running the bases. When he neared second, he hit the dirt and—headfirst, belly down, hands outstretched—slid until his fingers touched the base. Then he stood up, dusted off his shirt, and took off for third. This time, he slid feetfirst.

"What a weird way to spend your afternoon," Jason thought, shaking his head.

When he got home, he sat at the table, opened his library book, and began to read it again.

After an hour, his mind was swimming with information. He let his head fall with a thump on the table. "No way," he said to the tabletop.

That's how his mother found him when she came into the kitchen. She burst out laughing. "Goodness, Jason! What are you doing, getting a close-up look at your place mat?"

Jason lifted his head. She stopped laughing when she saw the look on his face.

"Is there something I can do to help?" she asked kindly.

"Got a magic potion that will turn me into an expert goalkeeper?"

Mrs. Shearer smiled and ruffled his hair. "Sorry, sport, but there's only one way you can get better at anything. Practice."

Jason's head thumped down again. He was still sitting like that when the phone rang. It was Dale.

"We're getting together for a pickup game of soccer tomorrow morning," he informed Jason. "Maybe you could come and work on your goalkeeping stuff."

"What goalkeeping stuff?" Jason said with a snort. But in the end, he agreed to play.

Several of the Soccer 'Cats were already at the field when Jason arrived the next morning. Stookie, Bundy, and Dewey were kicking a ball around while Lou, Amanda, Ted, and Lisa chatted. Dale showed up a few minutes later.

"Anyone else coming?" Bundy asked. "What about Bucky? He always shows up for these games."

"Not this time," said Dale. "He left for two weeks' vacation yesterday after practice."

"What!" Stookie cried. He put his hands on his hips. "So who's going to be our goalie?"

Everyone looked at Jason. Stookie rolled his eyes. "Oh, great. Mr. Comedian himself."

"Hey, give him a chance," Dale protested.

Bundy cut in. "There's nothing we can do about it, so let's just get on with the game," he said matter-of-factly. "There are nine of us, so how about three-on-three with goalies? I'll sit out until the first goal is made, then sub in for whoever made it."

The others agreed and chose up sides quickly. Stookie, Amanda, Dewey, and Jason were one team, with Lou, Dale, Lisa, and Ted as the other. Ted volunteered to play goalie.

"Are these teams fair?" Lisa wondered aloud as the teams took up positions. "Ted's never played goalie before."

Stookie booted a ball to her. "Trust me, they're fair. I mean, it's not like Jason knows what he's doing, either. Soccer's just a joke to him."

Chapter 5

Stookie's words stung Jason's ears. They hurt all the worse because Jason knew they were true. He hadn't been taking the Soccer 'Cats seriously. He was always clowning around during practices and wisecracking on the bench during games.

Now he wished he'd paid a little more attention. He tried to remember all the book had talked about, but everything was a jumble in his brain.

The pickup game started. Stookie and Amanda played the strikers against Lou and Dale. Lisa played defense opposite Dewey. Stookie and Lou did rock, paper, scissors to decide who'd start with the ball. Stookie won.

"Okay, here we go!" he cried. He set the ball down and tapped it to Amanda. Dale immediately tried to steal it from her, but Amanda was too quick. She dodged around him and took off down the field. When she saw Lou streaking toward her, she booted a pass to Stookie.

Stookie controlled the ball and made for the goal. Lisa came out to meet him. Stookie surprised her by belting the ball straight toward the goal. Ted made a feeble grab for it but missed.

Bundy came running onto the field as Stookie came running off. "Man, that was quick," Bundy said, slapping hands with his teammate as they passed each other. "If only it would be that easy against the Panthers!"

The two teams lined up again. Lou, Dale, and Lisa whispered together for a moment before Lou put the ball in play. He passed to Dale, then, instead of running downfield as Stookie had done, he dropped back behind Dale.

Confused, Bundy and Amanda both tried to follow Lou. Dewey ran up to challenge Dale. No one saw Lisa as she charged past Dale, but they all heard her when she yelled, "I'm open!"

Dale booted the ball to her. She caught it cleanly on her instep and turned to face the last obstacle on the field—Jason.

Okay, steady now, Jason thought. He tried to remember what the book had said about one-on-one situations. *Come out of the goal or stay in? Crouch down or spread arms and legs out to cover more area? Jump, slide, catch, punch, kick—what am I supposed to do?*

Lisa wound up and kicked. The ball came rocketing toward the goal like it had been

shot out of a cannon. Jason jumped, arms out-stretched, reaching for the ball—and missed.

"Oh, man," he heard Stookie groan from the sidelines. "He jumped *over* the ball! The game is going to be a *disaster!*"

Chapter 6

Jason stood up slowly, red-faced with embarrassment. As Stookie traded places with Lisa, Dale jogged up to Jason.

"Shake it off," Dale advised. "Try to remember what the book said to do."

"I *am*," Jason said glumly. "But it's all mixed up in my head."

"Hey, Dale, c'mon!" Amanda cried from midfield. "Let's get playing!"

Dale gave Jason one more encouraging look before he hurried back to his position.

The rest of the game was a blur. Jason tried, but he just couldn't seem to get anything right. When the ball was hit high, he jumped too soon—and could only watch as the ball soared over his fingertips as he landed. When it was a bouncing grounder, he lunged too late to stop it before it hit the back of the net. The only time he caught it was when it was kicked directly at his stomach. It hit him so hard he fell down, gasping for air.

As if that wasn't embarrassing enough, Stookie made sure Jason knew what he thought of his playing ability.

"I wonder if the scoreboard goes up to three thousand? 'Cuz that's probably how many goals the Panthers are going to score on Friday," he said after Jason muffed another easy shot on goal.

"Ball goes right, goalie trips over own feet and falls left," he cracked as Jason landed in the dirt. "You really showed 'em that time."

And when Jason crashed into the goalpost headfirst, Stookie just threw up his hands in disgust.

The other players gathered around Jason. "Are you okay?" Dale asked with concern.

Jason nodded, fighting back tears. He wasn't hurt, just totally humiliated.

"Course he's all right," Stookie said, bouncing the ball from one knee to the other. "The kid's head is made out of wood."

Dale whirled around, eyes blazing. He grabbed the ball away from Stookie and slammed it to the ground.

"Leave him alone, Stookie!" Dale cried. Stookie stared at him, astonished. The others, including Jason, looked equally surprised.

"C'mon Jason," Dale said, throwing an arm around his friend. "Let's go home."

Jason was too amazed to do anything but tag along with Dale. He had never seen his friend so steamed before!

"Gee, thanks, Dale," he said when they were off the field and walking by the playground.

Dale grinned at him. "Aww, it was nothing. But I sure would like to wipe that smug look off of Stookie Norris's face. Wouldn't it be great if you somehow turned into a good goalie by the game? That'd show him."

Jason walked along in silence for a moment. Then he stopped Dale. "Maybe—maybe, if you helped me, I *could* turn into a good goalie. Or at least, not a bad one."

"But where would we start?" Dale asked. "No offense, Jason, but you need help with everything."

"I know," Jason agreed glumly. "And there's so much to know, it's kind of overwhelming." He suddenly remembered the two kids he'd seen practicing baseball slides and rebounds. They'd looked a little silly to him at the time, but now Jason realized they were doing just what he should be doing—practicing the same thing over and over, one thing at a time.

He tugged at Dale's arm. "C'mon," he said. "We've got work to do!"

Chapter 7

Minutes later, Dale and Jason were in Jason's backyard. Jason had set out two chairs to act as the goal. A garden hose stretched on the ground between them represented the goal line. He had brought out the library book, too, and was reading through it.

"Okay," he said, closing the book. "First things first. There are three parts of the body I have to train—my hands, my eyes, and my feet. Hands for catching, eyes for watching the ball, feet for moving to and behind the ball."

"So how do we train those body parts?"

"I crouch down and hold my hands in a **W** like this." He demonstrated the catching position.

Dale nodded. "I've seen Bucky do that."

"You toss me some easy throws," Jason continued. "I catch them."

Dale picked up the ball. "Let's get started."

For the next ten minutes, Dale lobbed some soft tosses to Jason. Jason caught them easily. He signaled for Dale to start throwing harder. Dale did.

Jason caught some of them, but some he fumbled.

"Check your hand position," Dale advised. "I think it was wrong on that last catch."

After another fifteen minutes, Jason was doing better. "Let's move on to the next thing," he called to Dale. "You throw it next to me instead of right to me, and I try to get behind it."

"Are you going to dive for them?" Dale asked.

Jason shook his head. "Not yet. The book says it's a good idea to first learn to move my feet to get behind the ball."

On Dale's first throw, Jason tripped over the garden hose and fell flat on his face. Dale burst out laughing. Jason gave his friend a hurt look.

"Sorry," Dale said, still chuckling. "But I'm so used to laughing at you that it's hard to stop, even when I know you're being serious."

Jason toed the ball back to Dale. "I guess it's my own fault for being such a clown all the time," he admitted, not looking up. "I must really make people mad when I don't take the Soccer 'Cats seriously."

Dale dribbled up to him. "Maybe sometimes," he said. "But you know what? No one else on the team makes us laugh like you do. And soccer is supposed to be fun."

Jason broke into a lopsided grin. "Think that's what Stookie thinks?"

Dale returned his grin. "Does Stookie think at all? I wonder sometimes. He sure doesn't seem to think before he speaks."

Jason laughed. "Well, let's make him think twice about the things he said to me today. C'mon, let's take a break. My feet want to take me into the kitchen so my hands can wrap themselves around a sandwich."

"What are your eyes going to do?"

"They're going to watch you make my sandwich, of course!"

Cracking up, the boys raced into the house.

Chapter 8

During lunch, Dale and Jason looked through the soccer book together.

"Now I'll be able to coach you better," Dale said as he closed the book to finish his sandwich.

"Okay, Coach, what's our next move?" Jason said.

Dale gave him a stern look and pointed to the lunch dishes. "Clean up this mess. Then back to work!"

And work is just what they did, that afternoon and for the next two days.

Jason tried hard to improve. He took it one step at a time, working to master one skill before moving on to the next.

Dale was a good coach. When a hard kick rolled between Jason's legs, Dale reminded him to keep his feet together.

Once, he pointed out that Jason seemed to be too close to the garden hose.

"Didn't the book say to be sure to stay farther in front of the goal line? You know, so that you have room to take a step back if you need to, and so the ref knows for sure the ball was caught out of the goal?"

Jason nodded and moved forward a few paces.

By Wednesday afternoon, Jason felt ready to try some harder saves.

"Try kicking one up to the corner," he called to Dale. Dale did.

Jason jumped high and to the left, arms outstretched. He missed the ball by a foot.

"Rats," he said, discouraged.

"Hey, it's only your first try," Dale reminded him. "It took you three days of practice just to get good at easy saves. It's going to take more practice to get good at harder ones."

Jason sighed. "I know. It's just that there's hardly any time left before the game!" He sat down on one of the goal chairs. "And there's something else, too. I'm okay when it's just you and me. But what if I choke during a game, when I'm being swarmed?"

Dale sat on the other chair. "Good point. We should get more guys to help you work on that."

"When? There's only one day left before the game with the Panthers!"

"So we use that day as best we can." Dale stood up. "You call half the Soccer 'Cats tonight, and I'll call half. Tell them to meet at the field first thing tomorrow."

"What if they don't want to?"

Dale smiled. "Then tell them they have a choice. They can have a decent goalie on the field against the Panthers — or they can have the Master of Disaster!"

Chapter 9

The Soccer 'Cats all agreed to show up. Jason went to bed smiling.

But the next morning, his smile vanished as he heard the worst sound in the world: rain.

The soccer field is probably one big, giant mud puddle, Jason thought as he poked at his cereal. *So much for today's practice.*

He emptied his bowl into the sink and headed to the living room to watch TV. He was flicking through the channels when the doorbell rang. It was Dale, smiling out from

under the hood of a raincoat. He was carrying a soccer ball.

"Put on your rattiest pair of sneakers and an old sweatshirt and shorts," he said. "The team's waiting for you."

Too astonished to protest, Jason did as he was told. Five minutes later, he was at the soccer field with the rest of the 'Cats. They were all wearing their most worn-out clothes and sneakers—and were dripping wet from head to toe.

Jason started laughing. "Am I in the right place? I'm looking for the Soccer 'Cats—not the Drowned Rats!"

As everyone laughed, Stookie Norris suddenly picked up a ball and fired it at Jason. Jason caught it cleanly and held it tight against his chest, just as the book had instructed. Stookie raised his eyebrows.

"Not bad," he said. "Maybe tomorrow's game won't be such a disaster, after all."

"Let's split into defense and offense," Bundy

suggested, "and give Jason a taste of what that game might be like."

"It'll taste like victory!" Dale cheered. He pumped his fist in the air with such enthusiasm that he lost his balance and fell face first into the mud.

"Bet it'll be better than what *you* just got a taste of," Jason drawled. Everyone laughed, then headed for the field.

Lou, Stookie, and Dale took up offensive positions on the midfield line. Amanda, Dewey, and Bundy backed them up. Playing defense with Jason were Lisa, Ted, Alan Minter, and Edith "Eddie" Sweeny.

"All set, Jason?" Bundy called.

"Let 'er rip!" came Jason's reply.

Stookie placed the ball on the ground, then toed it to Lou. Lou took off for the goal. Lisa and Ted double-teamed him and tried to steal the ball. But Lou passed back to Dewey, who passed it to Dale.

Dale dribbled a few feet, dodged around

Alan, then booted the ball as hard as he could toward the goal.

Jason was ready. He uncoiled from his crouch, hands held in the W position, and stopped the ball cold.

"Whoa!" exclaimed Eddie. "Nice save!"

Jason grinned and lobbed the ball back to the forward line.

This time, Lou started the play by kicking the ball back to Bundy. Bundy immediately returned it to Lou, who dribbled furiously down the sideline. Ted and Lisa were on him again, but Lisa slipped and fell in the mud. Lou barreled on toward the goal.

Jason shifted from foot to foot, hands ready. Lou unleashed a powerful shot aimed at the left side of the goal. Jason moved sideways and got his body behind the ball. He didn't catch it, but he did deflect it so that it bounced harmlessly away.

Bundy scooped it up. "Two for two," he

said. "Good job." He tossed the ball back to the forward line.

The practice continued. Jason saved about half the shots on goal. He was covered with mud, but he didn't care. His hard work was paying off!

"Bucky better be careful," Lisa commented after a blocked shot, "or he'll be out of a job."

"Oh, really? Who's taking my job?"

Jason whirled around. There behind the net stood Bucky.

Chapter 10

"Hey, look who's here!" Lisa yelled.

"We thought you were on vacation," Bundy said as the rest of the Soccer 'Cats gathered around.

"My mom got called back on business, so we had to come home," Bucky answered. He looked at his mud-covered teammates and shook his head. "Sure am glad I missed this practice."

"Jason's been learning how to play goalie," Dale said. "He's getting pretty good, too."

"But now that you're back," Stookie cried,

"we won't need him! Look out, Panthers, here we come!"

Bucky grinned and all the Soccer 'Cats cheered — all, that is, except Jason and Dale. Dale tried to put an arm around Jason, but Jason shrugged him off. He walked off the field and headed for home.

Who needs 'em? he thought as he slogged through the rain. *All they care about is winning.*

A car horn beeped and startled him out of his dark thoughts. He looked up to see Coach Bradley leaning out of a car window.

"I thought that was you, Jason," the coach said. "C'mon, I'll give you a lift home."

Jason got in the car, buckled his seat belt, and slumped down in the seat.

"How'd you get so muddy?" the coach asked.

Jason hesitated. If he told the truth, the coach would surely figure out that he'd lied to him about knowing how to play goalkeeper. He was pretty sure the coach didn't like liars.

But what would it matter? Now that Bucky was back, Jason would be riding the pine, anyway. So he told the coach how he'd been practicing his goalkeeping skills to get ready for the game against the Panthers.

Coach Bradley looked astonished. "In the rain?" he said, eyebrows raised. "Why?"

"I didn't want to let the team down," Jason answered. "But hey, Bucky's back, so I guess you won't have to change the starting lineup, after all. What a relief."

The coach looked sideways at Jason. "No, I guess I won't." He pulled into Jason's driveway and put the car into park. "See you tomorrow, Jason."

Jason ducked out of the car before the coach could see his tears.

Jason almost didn't go to the game the next day. He didn't want to see how happy everyone was to have Bucky back. But Dale showed up at his house fifteen minutes before the game and convinced him to go.

"And bring your goalie shirt," Dale added.

"Oh, good idea," Jason said sarcastically. "It'll make a nice cushion to sit on while I'm on the bench. Or if it rains, I can use it for an umbrella. Or how about a hat if it's too sunny?"

"Just bring it," Dale insisted.

The first people Jason saw when they reached the field were Coach Bradley and Bucky. Coach Bradley was patting Bucky on the back and smiling broadly.

"Bet he's feeling lucky to have his goalie, Bucky," Jason said with a half-laugh, half-snort. "Get me. I'm a poet and don't know it." Dale shook his head.

Coach Bradley called for attention. "Let's get ready for warm-ups. But first, here's the starting lineup." As he read the roster, Jason listened with half an ear. It was the same as

usual—Lou, Stookie, and Jerry at forward, Amanda, Dewey, and Bundy at halfback, Ted, Lisa, Alan, and Brant at fullback. Then he heard something that made him sit up. "And because he's worked so hard all week, I'm starting Jason in the goal."

As the rest of the Soccer 'Cats cheered, Jason sat stock-still, dumbfounded.

"Hey, he's finally quiet, for once in his life!" Dale said with a laugh.

Stookie joined in. "We better hope he finds his tongue soon—after all, isn't that his tried-and-true method for goalkeeping?"

Jason popped a piece of gum in his mouth and grinned. "Nah, that was someone else's method—a guy I like to call the Master of Disaster! But he's going to sit on the bench this game while I show him how real goalkeepers do their thing!"